CHAPTER 1
OLYMPIC FEST

In the locker room before gym class, Kyle pulled his gym clothes out of his locker. He gave his T-shirt a quick sniff. *Gross*, he thought. *Guess it's time to take this home and wash it.*

Once he was dressed, he headed into the gym to meet the rest of his class.

His friend Ryan was waiting for him.

"Let's go," Ryan said. "We're meeting in the gym today instead of outside."

"Why?" Kyle asked. "We're not done with the soccer unit until next week, right?"

Ryan shrugged. "No clue," he said. "I just heard we're supposed to meet in the gym."

Kyle pulled open the creaky gym door. He was surprised to see a section of the bleachers pulled out. Everyone was sitting down. Mrs. Fitch, the gym teacher, stood next to a dry-erase board.

"Do you think we're in trouble?" Kyle whispered.

"You should be in trouble for how bad your clothes stink," Ryan whispered back.

"Nice," Kyle replied.

Kyle and Ryan walked up the bleacher stairs and took seats in the last row. Mrs. Fitch wrote OLYMPIC FEST in bold red letters on the chalkboard.

TABLE OF CONTENTS

"As most of you know, the Summer Olympics are coming up," Mrs. Fitch explained. "This year, we've decided to organize our own Olympic-themed unit here at Ring Lake."

"Cool," Ryan whispered. Ryan loved all sports, but Kyle wasn't sure how he felt about this. *Baseball and soccer are fun, but Olympic events?* Kyle thought. *No, thanks.*

"Immediately following our soccer unit," Mrs. Fitch continued, "we'll begin training for the Olympic Fest. The event will take place two weeks from Saturday. We'll be doing as many events as we can. But we'll treat this like the real Olympics. Each student will participate in one event."

"I want to do pole vaulting," Ryan whispered.

"You don't know how to pole vault," Kyle replied.

"Not yet," Ryan said, grinning.

"I've arranged for us to compete against four other schools," Mrs. Fitch said. "Each school will be like a different nation, competing for gold, silver, and bronze."

Medals? Kyle thought. He took a deep breath. *Maybe Olympic Fest is a bigger deal than I thought.*

Ryan raised his hand. "When do we pick our events?" he asked.

"Right now," Mrs. Fitch said. She held an upside-down football helmet filled with paper slips. "You'll each draw one."

CHAPTER 2
PICKED LAST

Kyle's classmates chattered with excitement as Mrs. Fitch shook up the slips in the helmet.

"As you may have guessed, we can't do all of the Summer Olympic events," Mrs. Fitch told the class. "Those of you hoping for sailing or equestrian will be disappointed."

Ryan leaned over to Kyle. "What's equestrian?" he asked.

"Horse stuff," Kyle replied. His older sister Rachel was crazy about horses.

"You'll come up one by one and choose a slip of paper," Mrs. Fitch instructed. "Once you've picked an event, please read it out loud, and I'll record it."

Starting with the first row, the kids in the class went to Mrs. Fitch and pulled their slips out of the helmet.

Alexa was first. "Badminton," she said loud enough for everyone to hear. Mrs. Fitch wrote down Alexa's choice on her list.

"Badminton is in the Olympics?" Kyle mumbled to Ryan.

"I guess so," Ryan replied.

As the list of students and events grew, Kyle realized something. He would be the last one to pick.

I chose the wrong day to pick a seat in the last row, he thought.

Ryan got up to pick his slip. "Fencing," he said. He looked at Mrs. Fitch. "Is that like swords and stuff?" he asked.

Mrs. Fitch laughed. "Yes, something like that," she replied.

"That's awesome," Kyle said as Ryan came back to his seat.

Kyle stood up. Then he walked to the front of the room to pick the last event for Olympic Fest.

Mrs. Fitch was smiling as Kyle reached into the helmet and pulled out the last slip. The words TRACK AND FIELD were written on it.

"Oh, no," Kyle groaned. "Is this hurdles and stuff?"

"Look on the back," Mrs. Fitch said.

Kyle flipped the paper over. The word THROWING was written on the back.

"You have the track-and-field throwing events," Mrs. Fitch explained. "Discus, javelin, shot-put, and hammer throw."

"Oh, cool," Kyle said.

"No fair," Ryan said when Kyle returned to his seat. "The throwing events are the coolest. Much better than fencing."

"Swords are pretty cool, too," Kyle said.

"They're called foils," Ryan said. "According to Mrs. Fitch."

"Whatever," Kyle replied.

Maybe this Olympic Fest thing will be cool after all, Kyle thought.

CHAPTER 3
FIRST TRIES

A week later, athletes and teachers from the participating schools came to Ring Lake Middle School. The students in different events would be practicing together several times a week leading up to the Olympic Fest.

Mrs. Fitch started the outdoor events first. When she had the runners and cyclists all set up, she headed over to Kyle and the rest of the track-and-field athletes.

Kyle glanced at the other athletes. He recognized one boy, Sam, from his math class. Kyle waved and made his way over.

"Hey, how's it going?" Sam asked.

"Okay," Kyle replied. He studied the items lying on the ground. There was a round, heavy-looking ball; a long spear; what looked like a metal Frisbee; and a ball attached to a wire and handle.

How hard can it be? Kyle thought.

"Okay, everyone," Mrs. Fitch said. "I'll be coaching your group. You get to participate in my favorite events from the Summer Olympics. The throwing challenges are extremely tough."

Mrs. Fitch hefted the handle for one of the throwing instruments. It looked like a steel softball attached to a metal wire.

"This is the hammer," Mrs. Fitch explained. "Make sure no one is standing around you before you get ready to throw."

Mrs. Fitch motioned for the students to back up. Once they were clear, she spun the hammer around her head twice, then spun herself around three times really quickly.

With a yell, Mrs. Fitch let go of the hammer. The group gasped as the hammer flew from her hands. It flew out into the field before landing and kicking up a swatch of dirt.

"Wow," Kyle said. "That looks tough."

A big guy smirked. "Yeah, right. Maybe for you," he said.

Sam shook his head. "That's Trevor," he whispered. "Just ignore him. I've heard he's really competitive."

"Yeah," Kyle said. "I guess."

Mrs. Fitch had each athlete come up and try the hammer throw. It was difficult for almost everyone. One student got tangled up and fell down. Another threw it about four yards. Trevor threw it the farthest, as if it were easy.

"Your turn, Kyle," Mrs. Fitch said, handing him the hammer.

Kyle took a deep breath and twirled the ball around his head. Remembering how Mrs. Fitch had done it, he lowered it so that his whole body spun around.

"That's it," Mrs. Fitch called.

Kyle suddenly felt dizzy. He tried to concentrate on letting go at the right time. He released the handle. Then he heard the rest of the track-and-field athletes gasp.

CHAPTER 4

PRACTICE MAKES PERFECT?

"Everybody, look out!" Mrs. Fitch shouted.

Kyle heard a loud clanging sound, like metal hitting metal. The noise rang out over the football field.

Then Kyle saw what had happened. He'd thrown the hammer into the bleachers. The metal ball rolled down the steel steps, making loud, clanking noises the entire time.

"Smooth," Trevor said. "Way to go, dork." He clapped slowly, and a couple of the other kids laughed.

"I'm so sorry, Mrs. Fitch," Kyle said.

"Now you know why there are nets around the circle at the Olympics," Mrs. Fitch said. "Let's move to the next event."

Mrs. Fitch picked up a flat metal disc. Kyle thought it looked like a miniature flying saucer.

"This is the discus," she said, holding it up for everyone to see. "Discus throw has been an event since the very first Olympic Games back in 1896. The ancient Greeks have thrown these around since 708 B.C."

"Wow," one of the students said. "I didn't know they had Frisbees back in ancient times."

Mrs. Fitch laughed. "Well, it's heavier than a Frisbee," she said. "The discus weighs more than four pounds for the men's competition and a little more than two pounds for women."

"Do you throw it like a Frisbee?" Kyle asked.

Trevor turned around and gave him a dirty look. "Haven't you ever watched the Olympics? What a dumb question," Trevor muttered.

"It's similar. The discus is held underneath the arm, though." Mrs. Fitch said. "Like the hammer, you spin and release it."

Mrs. Fitch launched the disc. Everyone had a chance to try it, too. Kyle was able to throw it without any problems.

Next Mrs. Fitch pointed to the metal ball on the ground. "The shot-put," she said.

Kyle nodded. He'd seen this event a few times on television. It seemed like the ball could be thrown like a baseball, but it was too heavy. The Olympic athletes just appeared to push it away from themselves.

Mrs. Fitch picked up the ball. She held it near her ear. Then she raised her free hand and arm up. She spun twice and pushed the heavy ball out into the field with a yell. It thumped down into the grass.

"There's a lot of spinning in track-and-field throwing events," Kyle said.

Mrs. Fitch brushed her hands off and nodded. "There is in three of them," she said. "But in the last event, you won't have to spin around at all."

CHAPTER 5
A NATURAL

The track-and-fielders were excited to
see Mrs. Fitch walk over to the area set up
for javelin throw next. She leaned down
and picked up the javelin.

The javelin reminded Kyle of an
enormous toothpick. The spear was at least
eight feet long and skinny. It was white and
had a blue stripe painted down one side.

At least this one can't weigh very much,
Kyle thought.

"The javelin throw is different from the other throwing events," Mrs. Fitch explained. "For the shot-put, hammer, and discus, you have to stay within a circle to make your throw. With the javelin, you run almost a hundred feet before throwing."

"Can you throw the javelin any way you want?" Sam asked.

"No," Mrs. Fitch said. "The javelin must be thrown overhand, and you can't twist your body. You'll need to hold it in the palm of your hand, high off the shoulder."

Mrs. Fitch placed the javelin in the palm of her hand to demonstrate. Then she ran smoothly toward a line in the grass, cocked her arm back, and threw.

The javelin sailed through the air and landed, sticking up from the ground.

"Nice," Kyle said. He couldn't wait to give it a try.

The students lined up to take turns. Everyone else seemed to do pretty well. When it was his turn, Kyle remembered what Mrs. Fitch had said.

Palm of the hand, Kyle thought. *High off the shoulder.*

Kyle ran toward the line. The javelin flexed a bit with every step. As he got closer, he pulled his arm back. He stopped short of the line, planted his front foot, and threw as hard as he could.

The javelin left his hand and rose in an arc out toward the field. He could hear some of the other guys behind him cheer. After what seemed like a long time, the javelin dropped and stuck into the grass.

"Wow," Mrs. Fitch said. "Very good, Kyle. You're a natural."

Kyle turned and smiled. A couple of the other guys nodded and clapped. Trevor just sneered at him.

Kyle looked down. He'd come close to stepping over the line. "What happens if you step over the line in any of these events?" he asked.

"In the Olympics, that's a foul and won't count," Mrs. Fitch said. "In our Olympic Fest, if you step over the line or step outside of the circle, you'd be disqualified."

"Wow," Kyle said. "That'd stink."

"But just for that event, Kyle," Mrs. Fitch said. "And, instead of awarding a medal for each event, the gold will go to the best all-around track-and-field competitor."

Kyle looked around. From the looks on the other boys' faces, he could tell they didn't know what she meant either.

"The scoring works like this," Mrs. Fitch explained. "Each event will be scored on a scale of one to five. Five points for the best, four points for second, and so on. The highest total score gets the gold medal."

"So a twenty is perfect," Trevor said. He looked confident, as if he already had the gold medal in the bag. "Fives across the board."

Great, Kyle thought. *I'm only good at one event. There goes my shot at the gold.*

CHAPTER 6
A FAIR TRADE?

At lunch, Kyle sat with Ryan.

"How'd the track-and-field stuff go?" Ryan asked. He took a big bite of his slice of cafeteria pizza.

"It was okay," Kyle said. "I need a lot more practice, though. I really screwed up some of the events. I just wish I could work on this stuff without everyone watching."

"Who says you can't?" Ryan replied through a mouthful of cheese and sauce.

"I don't exactly have a shot and a discus sitting around the house," Kyle said.

Ryan opened his carton of milk and turned to Kyle. "So ask Mrs. Fitch if you can use the stuff here," he said. "Simple."

"I don't know if she'll let me," Kyle said.

"Well, you won't know if you don't ask," Ryan said. "I'll help you practice throwing if you help me with my fencing."

"I don't know anything about fencing," Kyle said. "I don't even have a sword."

"It's a foil," Ryan corrected him. "And you don't need your own. You just need to pretend to be my opponent."

Kyle looked up at the ceiling. He really wanted to do better than Trevor. If he hoped to come close to winning, Kyle knew he'd have to practice outside of gym class.

There was no other choice.

"Deal," Kyle said, shaking Ryan's hand. "I'll ask Mrs. Fitch if we can use the throwing stuff. When do I get to be your pincushion?"

"Tomorrow after school," Ryan said. "It'll be great."

CHAPTER 7
PINCUSHION

Ryan was already waiting when Kyle arrived at the football field the next day. He held two big white masks with screens over the faces. There were two strange white shirts lying on the ground.

"Are those straitjackets?" Kyle asked, pointing at the shirts.

"No," Ryan said. "They're fencing jackets. Did Mrs. Fitch say you could use the track-and-field equipment?"

"Yeah," Kyle said. "I'm just supposed to get the gear out of the equipment shed and lock it up when we're done."

"Cool," Ryan said.

"I'm going to regret this," Kyle said as he slipped his arms into the white fencing jacket. "Please try not to poke holes in me."

Kyle barely had time to pull his helmet over his head before Ryan tossed him a foil.

"En garde!" Ryan shouted.

* * *

An hour and a half later, fencing practice was over. Kyle was relieved he'd made it through in one piece.

He and Ryan walked over to the equipment shed to get the track-and-field gear.

"Here we go," Kyle said. He removed the lock on the door and pulled the crate of supplies outside. He pointed to the javelin along the wall, and Ryan grabbed it.

"Fencing is pretty cool," Ryan said, "but throwing one of these has to be the best."

Kyle nodded. "Yeah," he said. "I like the javelin. I think that's the one event I'm going to score big on."

They dragged the gear to the middle of the football field. The circle Mrs. Fitch had sprayed into the grass was still there.

"The nice thing about practicing here is that I'll be able to tell how many yards I toss these things," Kyle said.

Ryan jammed the javelin into the ground. "Okay," he said. "So what am I supposed to do?"

Kyle picked up the twelve-pound shot and hefted it in his hand. "I just need you to watch my feet in the circle," he told Ryan. "Make sure I don't step out of bounds, no matter what. If I step out I'm disqualified for that event."

"Sheesh," Ryan muttered. "No do-overs?"

"No do-overs," Kyle said.

Ryan pulled the javelin from the ground and stood off to the side. He crouched down and waited, watching Kyle get ready to throw the shot.

"Is that thing heavy?" Ryan asked.

"Yes," Kyle replied. "Now don't talk. I have to concentrate."

"Sorry," Ryan whispered.

Kyle laughed and got into position. He tried to remember how many times he could spin without hopping out of the circle. He took a deep breath and spun once, twice, three times.

With a grunt, he heaved the shot into the air. It arced nicely, then landed with a thump nine yards away.

"You went over the line," Ryan said. "Or out of the circle thing, I mean."

Kyle looked down. Ryan was right. His left foot was clearly outside the circle. He was going to need more practice if he hoped to beat Trevor. Lots of practice.

CHAPTER 8

THE RIVAL RETURNS

That week, Kyle spent every afternoon at school practicing for Olympic Fest. Even when Ryan had to go home, Kyle stayed until he could no longer see the lines on the football field.

He could tell his technique was improving a little. For instance, he figured out that he could only spin twice when throwing the shot without stepping out of the circle.

He was still struggling with the hammer throw, though. No matter how he tried, Kyle couldn't manage to throw it straight.

One time the hammer slammed heavily into the equipment shed. Kyle cringed. He was pretty sure the entire neighborhood had heard the noise.

* * *

The next morning in gym class, all of the athletes from the other schools were there to practice — including Trevor.

Kyle and Sam stood together, waiting for practice to begin. Then Trevor walked over.

"Give up yet?" Trevor asked. "Or are you still throwing the hammer into the crowd?"

"Just keeping it interesting," Kyle replied. He tried not to let Trevor see how nervous he was.

Trevor gave him a dirty look and walked to where the hammer lay on the ground. He picked it up and shoved his way to the circle. He nudged Sam out of the way.

"Watch it," Sam shouted.

Trevor just shook his head. "No," he replied. "Watch this."

With perfect form, Trevor spun the hammer over his head twice. Then he swung it low, spinning on the tips of his toes, before releasing it.

The hammer sailed in a perfect line. Even Kyle was impressed. When the hammer finally landed, it was at least 35 yards away from them.

"Wow," Sam said. "He's even better."

"Yeah," Kyle replied. "And he was already pretty good."

Trevor high-fived some of the other guys and walked back over to where Kyle stood. He pointed toward the field where the hammer lay.

"Your turn," Trevor snarled.

Kyle nodded. "Nice throw," he said. He walked across the field to retrieve the hammer. Kyle wasn't a fan of Trevor's, but he meant it. The throw had been great. It would be almost impossible to beat Trevor, but Kyle had to try.

Once Kyle had the hammer, he took his spot in the circle. He could hear Trevor whispering something to the other guys, but he tried to block it out.

He's just trying to mess with me, Kyle thought. *I have to ignore him. Focus on the throw.*

Kyle spun the hammer around his head, trying to keep his focus on the far end of the field. He continued spinning around as he brought the hammer down.

Just as he was about to release the hammer, he heard Trevor shout.

"Look out, everyone, Kyle's about to throw!" Trevor yelled.

It was enough to break Kyle's focus, and his legs buckled. He let go of the hammer and fell to the ground. The hammer landed about five feet from the circle.

"Nice try," Trevor shouted. Kyle heard some of the other guys laugh.

Kyle stood up and shook his head. "At least I've got the javelin," he whispered. No matter what, he was going to beat Trevor at the javelin.

CHAPTER 9

SAM'S ADVICE

Friday was Kyle's last chance to practice before the Olympic Fest. He went to the football field after school to set up the track-and-field equipment.

"Hey," Sam called. "Wait up."

Kyle looked over his shoulder and saw Sam jogging toward him. He was carrying his tennis racket, and he looked sweaty.

"How's it going?" Sam asked. He flopped to the ground and swatted at a dandelion.

Kyle shrugged. "Okay, I guess," he said. "I figure I'll do well in javelin and middle of the road on shot-put and discus. But at the rate I'm going, I might end up getting disqualified for the hammer throw."

"Let me see you throw the hammer," Sam said.

"All right, but stand back," Kyle warned. "I never know where this thing is going to land."

Kyle concentrated. He began to spin around in the circle and pick up speed. When he thought he was lined up to throw straight down the field, he let go. The hammer arced left and flew into the running lanes of the track surrounding the field.

"Wow," Sam said. "That's . . ."

"Not good," Kyle finished for him. "I know."

"You're strong enough to throw it," Sam said. "Your timing is just off."

"Oh, really?" Kyle asked. He felt annoyed. How would Sam know?

"Yeah," Sam said. "When are you letting go of the handle?"

Kyle took a deep breath and looked out to where the hammer had landed. Then he turned and glanced down toward the goal posts at the other end of the football field.

"I don't know," he said. "I guess when it looks like I'm lined up with where I want to throw it."

Sam nodded. "So what about letting go sooner?" he suggested. "Try letting go of the hammer a quarter-turn early."

Kyle got ready to try again. He tried to throw it like Sam had suggested. The hammer went off to the left again.

"See?" Kyle said. "I told you. Nothing helps."

"Okay," Sam said. "Let go even earlier this time."

Kyle threw the hammer again and again. Each time it went a little straighter.

Maybe he's right, Kyle thought. But he still couldn't make it perfect.

Kyle sighed. "Thanks for the advice," he said. "But I might just have to accept that Trevor's got the hammer throw in the bag."

"Don't say that," Sam said. "You have to at least try to beat him on every event, even the one you like the least."

Kyle held up the hammer. "Well, this is the one," he said.

Sam picked up his tennis racket and turned around. "What are you doing later?" he asked. "Want to come over and play video games or something?"

"Nope," Kyle replied. "If I want to have a shot at beating Trevor, I need to practice until I can't do it anymore."

"Wow," Sam said. "You must really want to beat this guy."

You have no idea, Kyle thought.

CHAPTER 10
OFF TO A BAD START

The next morning, as Olympic Fest was about to start, Kyle stood at the end of a narrow lane, holding the javelin.

Sam ran up to him. "How do you feel?" he asked.

"Tired," Kyle said. His arms felt like spaghetti from practicing so much, and he'd hardly slept the night before.

"Javelin is your best event," Sam reminded him. "Start it off with a bang."

Kyle nodded and looked around. The football bleachers were full of parents, friends, and relatives.

Okay, Kyle thought. *Time to see if all that practice paid off.*

"Are you ready?" an official asked. He stood off to one side, a whistle in his hand.

"I think so," Kyle said. The official nodded and blew the whistle.

It was time. Kyle raised the javelin up, making sure to carry it in the palm of his hand. He focused on the field ahead of him and ran. Every footstep seemed extra loud. It felt like all eyes were on him.

As he ran toward the line, Kyle pulled his arm back, ready to launch the javelin. He planted his foot and threw.

Then a whistle blew.

"Foul!" an official near the line shouted, a whistle in her mouth. Kyle watched the javelin fly through the air anyway.

It was a great throw. Or it would have been. Kyle looked down. His foot had crossed the foul line.

Kyle got a zero for the javelin throw. He walked over to his group of athletes. He wasn't surprised to see Trevor grinning.

"Keep doing that," Trevor said. "You'll make it even easier for me to win."

Kyle watched as the rest of the guys threw. Only one other athlete fouled. It didn't make Kyle feel any better

It didn't surprise Kyle that Trevor threw the javelin farther than everyone else. Everyone, that is, except Kyle. But because of his foul, it didn't matter.

"Shake it off, man," Sam called from the sidelines. "There are still three more events. You can still score a medal!"

I doubt it, Kyle thought. But then he thought about the past two weeks. He'd skipped his favorite TV shows and ignored his video games to practice. He'd worked too hard to give up now.

The shot-put was next. Kyle went last. He held the ball close to his ear, extended his arm like a pro, and spun cleanly twice. The shot flew in a nice arc and landed farther away than any of the others.

Trevor gave him a dirty look. "Lucky throw," he said.

"Not really," Kyle replied. Then he prepared himself for the next event.

CHAPTER 11
HAMMER TIME

"The hammer throw must be last," Sam said to Kyle. The officials had just brought a discus to the circle.

"Good luck," Sam said. "I hope you beat Trevor."

"Yeah, me too," Kyle said.

But Kyle wasn't sure anyone could beat Trevor. In every group practice, Trevor had thrown the hammer farther than anyone else.

Don't worry about the hammer throw, Kyle told himself. *Focus on the discus. You need to do well on all the events, especially now.*

Sam threw first. Kyle was last. When it was his turn, he took his position in the circle and held the discus tightly under his arm. He took a deep breath as he wound up.

An official stood outside the circle. "Ready?" he asked.

Kyle nodded, and the whistle blew.

Kyle swung his arm back and forth twice to start his turn. On the third twist, he spun twice and launched the discus into the air. He hopped twice, coming dangerously close to stepping outside the circle.

The discus landed toward the middle of the pack.

"I think that's four points," Sam whispered to Kyle, clapping him on the shoulder. "You edged out Trevor in that one."

With three events done, Kyle looked at the white board set up along the edge of the bleachers. With only five athletes competing in the track-and-field events, it was easy to see how he was doing.

"Wow," Kyle said. "I've got nine points. That puts me in second place, even with my foul."

"I'm tied for third," Sam said. "I just have to get past the hammer throw."

Kyle sighed. "Me too," he said. If he threw the hammer like he usually did, Sam would get the silver medal. That would be okay. But Trevor would be guaranteed gold.

The athletes lined up for the final event. Kyle would throw second to last. Trevor, who was currently in first place, would throw the hammer last.

In no time, it was Kyle's turn. He felt nervous as he headed toward the circle.

"Hey, Kyle," Trevor called. "Don't throw it into the stands. There are people sitting there this time."

Kyle ignored him and grasped the hammer handle. He looked at the flags that marked the previous throws.

Last chance, Kyle thought. He hefted the hammer and nodded to the official.

The whistle blew, and Kyle began his swing.

Kyle spun the hammer twice around his head and turned perfectly within the circle.

Release earlier than where you're aiming,
Kyle thought. He saw the field at the edge of
his line of sight and let go.

As the handle left his hands, he closed
his eyes and kept his body inside the circle.
When he opened his eyes again, he saw the
hammer drop at the far end of the field,
past the farthest marker.

The crowd cheered. Kyle could hardly
believe it. He was in the lead.

He high-fived Sam as he came back to
the group. As Trevor made his way to the
circle, he slammed into Kyle's shoulder.

"Too little, too late," Trevor grumbled.

Kyle was too happy with his throw to let
Trevor ruin it. He suddenly realized it didn't
matter if Trevor ended up with the gold. The
silver medal was his, and he'd thrown the
hammer like a pro.

The official blew the whistle to signal Trevor's start.

Almost immediately, another whistle sounded, followed by the clank of the hammer hitting the ground.

Kyle turned. He turned and saw Trevor down on his knees outside the circle.

"That's a foul," the official called. "The contestant is disqualified for stepping outside the circle."

"Dude," Sam whispered. "I think you just won."

Kyle turned to look at the scoreboard. With his new score of five points for the hammer throw, Kyle's total was fourteen points. He'd beaten Trevor by two points.

Kyle knew what he had to do. He walked over to Trevor and held his hand out.

"What do you want?" Trevor asked. "Are you here to gloat?"

"No," Kyle said. "I came over to help you up."

Trevor took a deep breath. For a minute, Kyle thought the big guy would punch him in the stomach. Instead, Trevor took Kyle's hand and let Kyle pull him to his feet.

"Nice throw," Trevor said with a nod. "You deserved to win."

"Thanks," Kyle said. He shook Trevor's hand. "Now let's go get our medals."

ABOUT THE AUTHOR

Thomas Kingsley Troupe writes, makes movies, and works as a firefighter/EMT. He's written many books for kids, including *Legend of the Vampire* and *Mountain Bike Hero*, and has two boys of his own. He likes zombies, bacon, orange Popsicles, and reading stories to his kids. Thomas currently lives in Woodbury, Minnesota, with his super-cool family.

ABOUT THE ILLUSTRATOR

Eduardo Garcia has illustrated for magazines around the world, including ones in Italy, France, United States, and Mexico. Eduardo loves working for publishers like Marvel Comics, Stone Arch Books, Idea + Design Works, and BOOM! Studios. Eduardo has illustrated many great characters like Speed Racer, the Spiderman family, Kade, and others. Eduardo is married to his beloved wife, Nancy M. Parrazales. They have one son, the amazing Sebastian Inaki, and an astonishing dog named Tomas.

GLOSSARY

competition (kom-puh-TISH-uhn)—a contest of some kind

confident (KON-fuh-duhnt)—having a strong belief in your own abilities

disqualified (diss-KWOL-uh-fyed)—banned from taking part in an activity, often because a rule has been broked

discus (DISS-kuhss)—a large, heavy disk that is thrown in a track-and-field event

equipment (i-KWIP-muhnt)—the tools and machines needed for a particular purpose

javelin (JAV-uh-lin)— a light, metal spear that is thrown for distance in a track-and-field event

organize (OR-guh-nize)—to plan and run an event

participate (par-TISS-uh-pate)—to join with others in an activity or event

DISCUSSION QUESTIONS

1. Why do you think Trevor was so rude to Kyle during the competition? Talk about some possible reasons he acted the way he did.

2. If your school was hosting an Olympic Fest, what event would you want to compete in? Talk about what sport you would choose and why.

3. The track-and-field throwing category has several events. Which do you think is the most difficult: javelin, hammer throw, discus, or shot-put? Talk about your choice.

WRITING PROMPTS

1. Kyle was nervous to try a new sport that he wasn't good at. Write about a time you had to try something new. What was it? How did it turn out?

2. Kyle's friends helped him get ready for Olympic Fest throughout the story. Write about a time your friends helped you prepare for something.

3. Kyle thought that javelin would be his best event, but he ended up getting disqualified. Write about a time something turned out differently than you originally expected.

THROWING EVENTS

Many Olympic sporting events can be traced back to ancient times. Here's a look at how these events began:

JAVELIN

Javelin throwing dates back to prehistoric times, when it was used as a hunting tool. Records of a javelin competition in 708 B.C. show that there were two types: throwing at a target and throwing for distance. Today's modern javelin competitions are based on throwing for distance. The first Olympic javelin throw for men was held in 1908, and a women's event was added in 1932.

HAMMER THROW

The hammer throw can be traced back to 1800 B.C., when competitors threw a weight attached to a rope, a large rock attached to a wooden handle, or a chariot wheel on a wooden axel. The men's hammer throw, which uses a 16-pound metal ball, became an official Olympic event in 1900. The women's hammer throw, which uses an almost-9-pound ball, didn't become an Olympic event until 2000.

SHOT-PUT

Shot-put competitions can be traced back to pre-historic competitions with rocks, such as the "stone put" in Scotland in the middle ages. Modern shot-put rules were first created in 1860, and the sport was added as a men's Olympic event in 1896. A women's shot-put competition was added as an Olympic sport in 1948. The shot for men's competitions weighs 16 pounds, while the shot for women's competitions weighs almost nine pounds.

DISCUS

The history of the discus dates all the way back to 708 B.C. In ancient times, competitors stood in a set position on a small pedestal and threw a heavy disk. This style of throwing was used until the 1906 Olympics in Athens, when the more modern discus throw appeared. Today, athletes spin and throw the 4.4-pound, 8-inch discus, rather than throw from a standing position. In 1928, the women's discus became one of the first official Olympic events for women.